SARAH'S STORY

Bill Harley

Illustrations by
Eve Aldridge

TRICYCLE PRESS
Berkeley | Toronto

TRICYCLE PRESS
a little division of Ten Speed Press
P.O. Box 7123, Berkeley, California 94707
www.tricyclepress.com

Design by Mina Greenstein
Production by Katy Brown
Typeset in Versailles

Library of Congress Cataloging-in-Publication Data
Harley, Bill, 1954–
    Sarah's story / by Bill Harley ; illustrations by Eve Aldridge.
        p.   cm.
    Summary: Sarah cannot think of a story to tell in class for her homework
assignment, but on her way to school she gets help from some unexpected sources.
    ISBN-13: 978-1-883672-20-1 hc / ISBN-13: 978-1-58246-178-6 pbk
    ISBN-10: 1-883672-20-1 hc / ISBN-10: 1-58246-178-3 pbk
    [1. Ants—Fiction. 2. Bees—Fiction. 3. Schools—Fiction. 4. Storytelling—Fiction.]
    I. Aldridge, Eve, ill. II. Title.
    PZ7.H22655Sar 1996
    [E]—dc20   96-4274
                                                                    CIP
                                                                    AC

First printing, 1996
First paperback printing, 2006
Printed in Singapore
1 2 3 4 5 6 — 10 09 08 07 06

To Lily Susanna Shield, who already has a lot of stories.
—B.H.

For adventurers and dreamers and those who support them;
and, of course, Miles.
—E.A.

It was almost time to go home when Sarah's teacher said, "Class, tomorrow morning I'm going to have everybody tell a story. So think of a story you can tell."

"But I don't know any stories," Sarah complained.

"Sarah, everybody knows a story," her teacher said.

"Not me," grumbled Sarah.

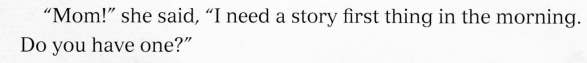

"Mom!" she said, "I need a story first thing in the morning. Do you have one?"

Sarah's mother was tired. "You used to love 'Goldilocks and the Three Bears.' Why don't you tell that?"

"Oh Mom!" Sarah said in her best grouchy voice, "Everybody knows that story! Thanks a lot."

At bedtime, Sarah still hadn't thought of a story.
She knew she couldn't, and she didn't. She tried
to think of a story when she woke up. She couldn't.
She tried to think of one at breakfast. She didn't.

On her way to school, Sarah stopped and waited for the light to change. She was still trying to make up a story when she heard the tiniest and squeakiest of voices say,

"Hey, Sarah! Hey! Down here!"

There, on the sidewalk, was an ant.

"Are you talking to me?" Sarah asked.

"Isn't your name Sarah? Come on." The ant turned and started down into an anthill.

"Wait one big minute," said Sarah, "I can't go down there. I'm a big girl and you're just a little ant."

"Let's go!" said the ant, and it disappeared down the hole.

Sarah knew she had to get to school, but an ant had never spoken to her before. The anthill wasn't very big, but it was a little bigger than anthills usually are. Besides, she wanted to show that she had tried. Sarah took off her shoes and socks, and put her big toe into the very corner of the hole.

She got part of that toe in, then she squeezed and *twisted,* and sucked in her breath as hard as she could.

FWOP!

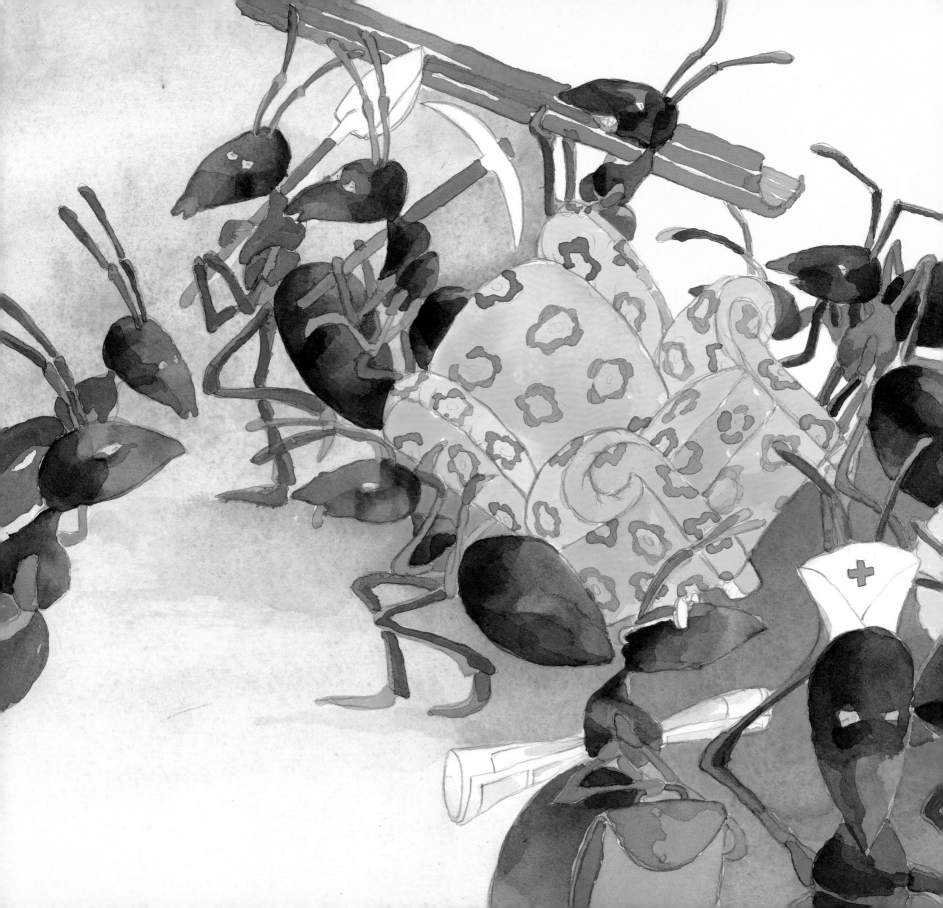

She was inside the anthill!
There were thousands of
ants swarming around,
mumbling and burbling.
She didn't know what they
were saying, but then,
she wasn't an ant.
"Come on," said the ant,
and
it started
down a long passageway.

Sarah followed the ant deep into the earth until they came to a little room. There, on the other side, was the queen ant. Sarah knew it was the queen because she was wearing a crown that said **"Queen"** on it.

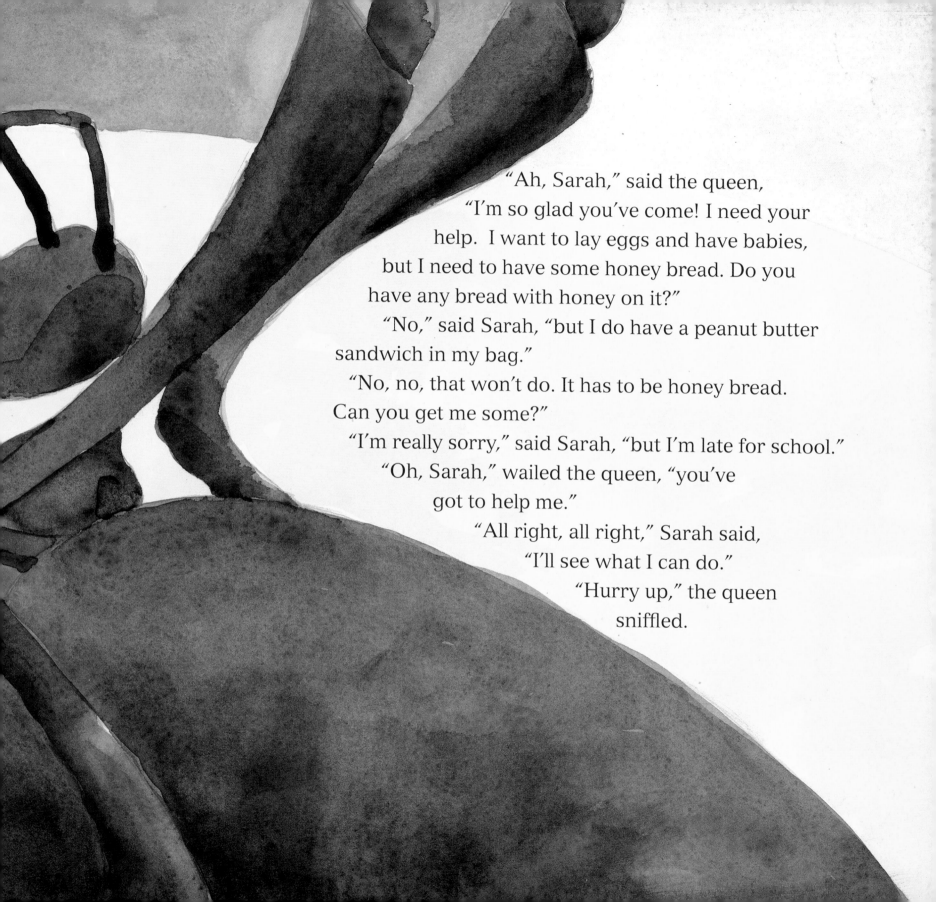

"Ah, Sarah," said the queen,
"I'm so glad you've come! I need your
help. I want to lay eggs and have babies,
but I need to have some honey bread. Do you
have any bread with honey on it?"

"No," said Sarah, "but I do have a peanut butter
sandwich in my bag."

"No, no, that won't do. It has to be honey bread.
Can you get me some?"

"I'm really sorry," said Sarah, "but I'm late for school."

"Oh, Sarah," wailed the queen, "you've
got to help me."

"All right, all right," Sarah said,
"I'll see what I can do."

"Hurry up," the queen
sniffled.

Sarah turned and ran. She squeezed her way out of the anthill and pulled herself back up on the sidewalk, right next to her shoes and socks.

"Where am I going to get some honey?" Sarah wondered.

As she thought about it, a bee buzzed around her head.

"Hi, Sssarrrahh. Climmbbb onnnn."

"Wait one big minute. I can't climb on you," said Sarah, "I'm a big girl and you're just a little bee."

"Climmbbb onnnn!" the bee ordered.

"This is ridiculous," muttered Sarah, but she put one leg on one side of the bee, then one leg on the other.

The bee took off! They zoomed across the street,
right by the school, over a field, and headed straight
for a huge beehive high up in a tree.

"*Oh nooo!*" Sarah screeched.

FWUMP!

They were inside the beehive. There were thousands of bees, swarming and buzzing. She didn't know what they were saying, but then, she wasn't a bee.

The bee opened up a honeycomb and honey dripped out. When Sarah's hands were full, the bee sealed the comb and said, "Climmbbb onnnn."

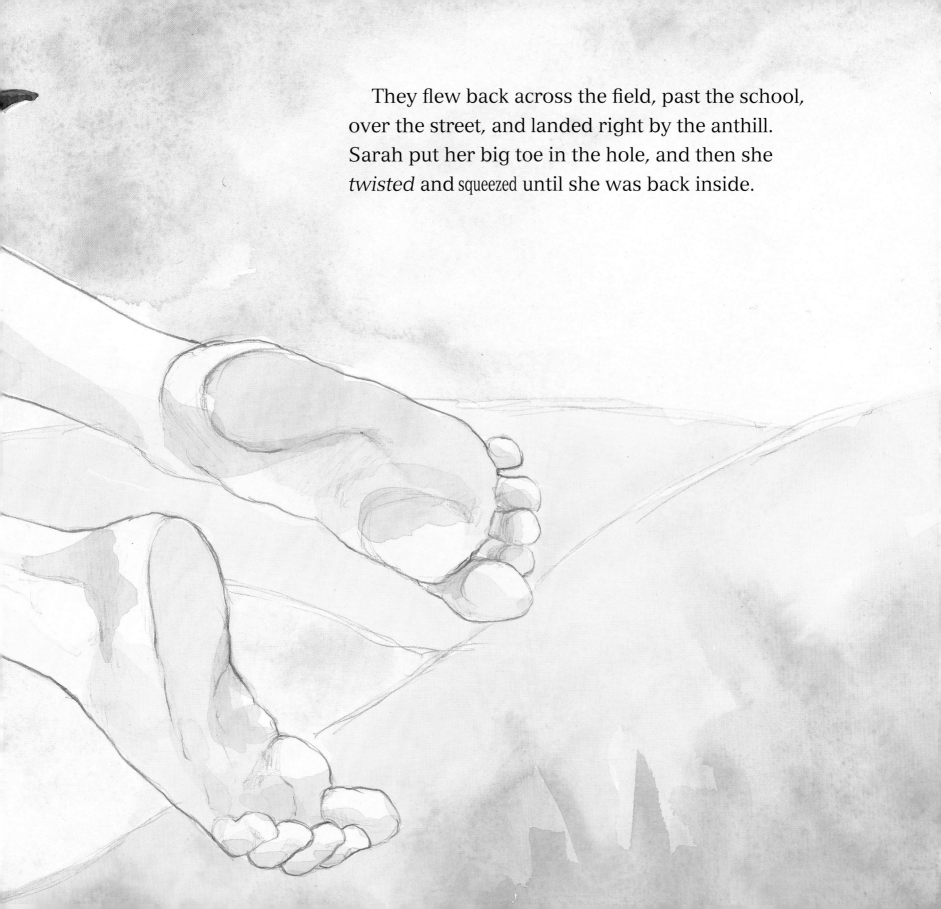

They flew back across the field, past the school, over the street, and landed right by the anthill. Sarah put her big toe in the hole, and then she *twisted* and squeezed until she was back inside.

Sarah ran down the passageway and into the queen's room. "I...I got the honey," she gasped.

"Good for you," said the queen. "Where's the bread?"

"Oh, no," said Sarah, "I forgot. Look, I'm already late for school. I've got this peanut butter sandwich. Why don't we just take the honey and put it on the peanut butter sandwich?"

"That won't do at all," said the queen.

"Why not?" asked Sarah.

"I don't like peanut butter," said the queen.

"Why not?"

"I don't like how it looks," sniffed the queen.

"Have you ever tried it?" asked Sarah.

"No."

"You have to try it," said Sarah. "One bite. **IT'S THE RULE.**"

Sarah took out the peanut butter sandwich, squeezed the honey on it, rolled it into a big sticky ball, and held it out to the queen.

"Yuck!" said the queen, but she took one little bite. **"WOW**, this is **FANTASTIC!"** she burbled, "Sticky, too. Sarah, you did it.

"I'm going to have a thousand babies and name them all after you. Let's see, I'll call them Sarah One, Sarah Two, Sarah Three, Sarah Four...."

"What are you doing?" asked Sarah.

"Counting to one thousand," said the queen.

"I've gotta go!" Sarah said, and she ran up the long passageway.

She pulled herself back up on the sidewalk and put
on her shoes and socks. She ran all the way to school,
raced down the hallway, burst into her classroom, and
plopped into her seat.

"Sarah," said her teacher, "you're late."

"I know," gasped Sarah, "I'm sorry. I got stuck."

"Well," her teacher said, "everyone here has told a story. Could you tell yours?"

"I don't have a story," Sarah said.

"Why not?" her teacher asked.

"Well, I couldn't think of one and I told you I couldn't and I didn't. I was trying to think of one when I was walking home from school, but I couldn't and I didn't think of one this morning. And I was walking to school and I was still trying to make up a story and this ant came along and wanted my help so I got my toe inside the anthill and the ants were burbling—I didn't understand them but I'm not an ant. And I ran down this long passageway to the queen's room and I knew it was the queen because she had a crown on her head that said 'Queen.' She wanted some honey bread and I tried to give her my peanut butter sandwich, and she was about to cry so I said I would help.

"I ran up the long passageway and got outside and was looking for some honey and a bee came along and we flew across the street and by the school and over the field right inside the beehive and I got all this honey on my hands.

"Then we flew back to the sidewalk, I squeezed down into the anthill again and ran down the long passageway.

"The queen said where's the bread and I said I don't have any and she said you have to get some and I said how about with a little peanut butter.

"She said she didn't like the looks of it, I said just one bite, it's the rule.

"She tried it, she liked it, and she's gonna have a thousand babies and name them all after me: Sarah One, Sarah Two…I said I gotta go!

"I ran up the long passageway, and I found my shoes, and I ran across the street. I ran in here and that's why I don't have a story."

And the kids in Sarah's class said, "NO WAY." Sarah said, "That's true. It's not a story!" Sarah's teacher smiled and said, "Sarah, true or not, that's the best story we've heard all day."

The end.